MARVEL

SUPER HERO
ADVENTURES

Mighty Marvels!

With Spider-Man, Captain Marvel,
Ms. Marvel, and the Green Goblin

By **Mackenzie Cadenhead**
& Sean Ryan

Illustrated by **Derek Laufman**

MARVEL

Los Angeles
New York

Dedication
For Lyra and Chachi Mini—MC
For Joanna, always—SR

MarvelHQ.com

Designed by David Roe
Painted by Anna Beliashova and Vita Efremova

Printed in the United States of America
First Paperback Edition, February 2019
10 9 8 7 6 5 4 3 2 1
Library of Congress Control Number: 2018961916
ISBN 978-1-368-00858-7
FAC-029261-18355

SUSTAINABLE FORESTRY INITIATIVE
Certified Sourcing
www.sfiprogram.org
SFI-01415

Spider-Man

Peter Parker was just a normal kid when he was bitten by a radioactive spider and became **The Amazing Spider-Man**! He has super strength, can climb walls, and can jump incredible distances. Being the science-minded kid that he is, Peter also made his very own web-shooters. Peter takes his job as a Super Hero seriously because of the lesson his Uncle Ben taught him: With great power comes great responsibility.

Captain Marvel and Ms. Marvel

Captain Marvel and **Ms. Marvel** are one powerful duo. Captain Marvel, also known as Carol Danvers, was given her astounding powers by aliens. She's superstrong, she can fly, she can shoot blasts of energy from her hands, and she can absorb energy, too. Working alongside Captain Marvel is Ms. Marvel. The hero, Kamala Khan, is a high school student from New Jersey who discovered that she has the amazing power to morph her body into anything she wants. She can stretch, elongate, shrink, or grow! Her idol has always been Captain Marvel. And now they save the world together!

The Green Goblin

The Green Goblin is Spider-Man's most feared foe. Behind the mask he is actually Norman Osborn, CEO of the company Oscorp. Wanting to be the most powerful person ever, Norman injected himself with a dangerous serum that gave him super smarts . . . but also made him crazy! With his knowledge of machines, he's built himself a flying glider and all sorts of things with which to cause trouble. He's been stopped by Spider-Man too many times to count, which is why he considers the web-slinger enemy number one!

Chapter 1

"Watch out!"

Peter Parker's eyes widened as he leaped over a dog.

"Thanks, MJ," he called over his shoulder to the red-haired girl who had issued the warning. He held her by the hand and pulled her along with him. Peter and his friend Mary Jane Watson skirted a sandwich board and raced past a pretzel stand. But despite the obstacles in their way, they didn't slow down. They ran. Fast.

New York's Coney Island was full of people enjoying the beautiful summer day. They strolled down the boardwalk. They rode the Ferris wheel. They lounged on the beach. Only Peter and MJ seemed in a hurry to get anywhere. Did Peter know something no one else did?

Thanks to his secret identity— Spoiler: Peter Parker is Spider-Man!— Peter often found himself rushing off to fight crime. Was the Sandman stealing all the sand on the beach? Had Doctor Octopus taken over the Aquarium?

"There it is!" Peter hollered. He dropped MJ's hand and sprinted the rest of the way to the Ford Amphitheatre. A banner that read THE FUTURE IS NOW SCIENCE EXPO hung above the entrance where a line was starting to form. Peter took his spot at the back of it and grinned.

"I can't believe we're going to see the Anti-Grav 500 in person!" he said. "A machine that can reverse the law of gravity to make objects weightless! Do you realize what this could do for micro-particle physics?"

"Or basketball," MJ joked as she joined him. She rested her hands on her knees and caught her breath. "I know you're excited, Pete, but couldn't we have stopped for just one hot dog at Nathan's?"

Peter rolled his eyes. "And risk not getting in?"

Mary Jane looked at the seven people ahead of them. "I don't think we have to worry about that."

"Why worry about anything?" a nearby voice asked.

Peter turned to see his friend Harry

Osborne exiting the Amphitheatre.
"Harry!" he said. "What are you doing
here?"

"My dad's company, Oscorp, is
sponsoring the Expo," Harry answered.
"I've been here all morning. Why don't
you guys hang with me backstage?"

"Do you have hot dogs?" MJ asked.

"Nathan's famous all-beef hot dogs? Of course," Harry replied.

MJ smiled. "That sounds—"

"Terrible," Peter interrupted. "I've been planning to come to this event for months. I planned to get in line early. I planned to make friends with my fellow line-goers—"

The kid beside them saluted. "What's up?"

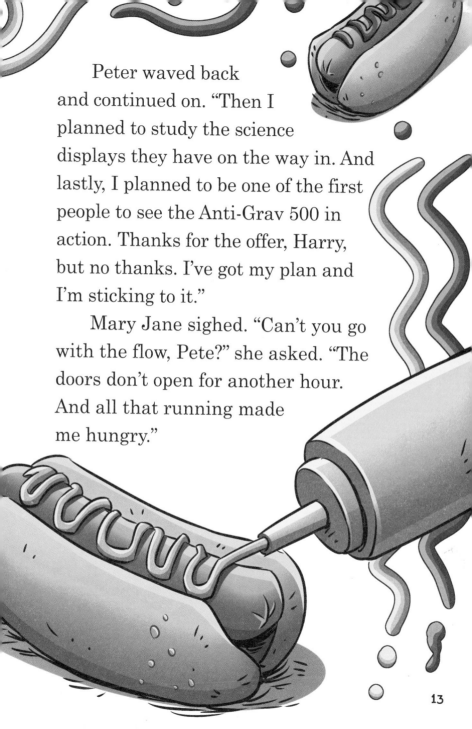

Peter waved back and continued on. "Then I planned to study the science displays they have on the way in. And lastly, I planned to be one of the first people to see the Anti-Grav 500 in action. Thanks for the offer, Harry, but no thanks. I've got my plan and I'm sticking to it."

Mary Jane sighed. "Can't you go with the flow, Pete?" she asked. "The doors don't open for another hour. And all that running made me hungry."

Peter's stomach growled. He ignored it and crossed his arms. "You can go if you want, but I'm staying put."

Mary Jane frowned. "Okay, well, text us if you change your mind."

Peter said nothing as MJ and Harry walked toward the Amphitheatre's backstage door. He turned to the guy in line who had saluted them, and was now eating a sandwich. "What've you got there?" Peter asked.

"Peanut butter, anchovy and mayonnaise," his line-mate answered. "Want some?"

Peter's stomach flipped and he covered his mouth. "You know, maybe I do have time for one hot dog," he said. Then he left the line and ran after his friends.

Chapter 2

The Anti-Grav 500 rested inside a glass case on the Amphitheatre's stage. Though right now the auditorium was empty, in less than an hour, hundreds of people would witness this modern marvel at work. Until then, a different kind of marvel had a job to do.

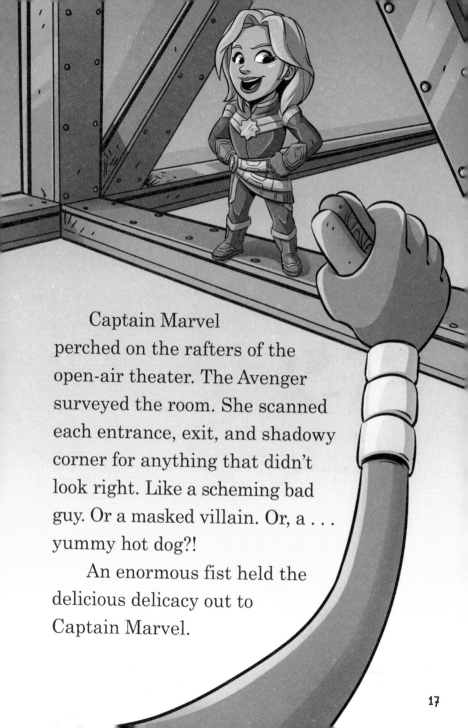

Captain Marvel perched on the rafters of the open-air theater. The Avenger surveyed the room. She scanned each entrance, exit, and shadowy corner for anything that didn't look right. Like a scheming bad guy. Or a masked villain. Or, a . . . yummy hot dog?!

An enormous fist held the delicious delicacy out to Captain Marvel.

"One Nathan's all-beef hot dog with the works," said a voice from the far end of the auditorium. It was Captain Marvel's friend and fellow Super Hero Kamala Khan, also known as Ms. Marvel. Her super-human stretchy arm delivered the food while the rest of her body caught up.

"Aw, you got me a snack?"
Captain Marvel asked.

"That I did!" Ms. Marvel
replied.

Captain Marvel licked her
lips. "You are my favorite Super
Hero," she said. She took a bite.

"I bet you say that to all the
Avengers," Ms. Marvel teased.

"Just the ones who feed me *and* save the day," Captain Marvel said between mouthfuls. "Speaking of day-saving, let's review the plan."

Ms. Marvel said, "We scan the sky!"

Captain Marvel nodded. "If Avengers intel is right, the Green Goblin is going to try to steal the Anti-Grav 500 today. Everything we know about him says he'll either fly in or out on his goblin glider. So I'll patrol the South horizon."

"And I've got the North," Ms. Marvel confirmed.

"Time to go to our posts," said Captain Marvel.

Ms. Marvel put her hands on her hips. "Aren't you forgetting something?"

Captain Marvel smiled. The heroes faced each other and commenced their secret handshake.

"Marvel me! Marvel you! Marvel US!" They chanted in unison.* Then Captain Marvel and Ms. Marvel separated. They took their positions and waited for the Green Goblin to strike.

*Wish you knew the Marvels' secret handshake? Well, you're in luck, True Believer! There's a Mighty Marvel Handshake How-To at the back of the book.

Chapter 3

"This is the only way I want to attend science expos from now on," Mary Jane said as she helped herself to a second hot dog. She, Harry, and Peter were in a room behind the auditorium. It was a private area filled with tasty treats and comfortable couches.

"It's fine, I guess," Peter said. He gnawed on a pretzel. "But I think we should get back to the line now."

"What?" Harry asked. "Peter, I brought you here so we could all hang out. That's the point."

Peter shook his head. "No. The point is to gain scientific knowledge!"

"You can do that, too," Harry assured. He pointed to a big-screen TV across from them. "When the presentation starts we can grab some popcorn and watch it on that monitor."

Peter's mouth fell open. "If I wanted to see the Anti-Grav 500 on a screen I could have stayed home and watched YouTube," he cried. He tossed the rest of his pretzel into the trash and shoved his hands in his pockets. "Leaving the line was a mistake. I'm going back. I'll see you guys later."

"Peter, wait," MJ called. But it was too late. Peter had left the room in search of an exit. Unfortunately, finding one was not easy.

"All these hallways look the same," Peter muttered to himself. He wandered around the mazelike corridors of the Amphitheatre's backstage for a few minutes before he finally saw a sign that read STAGE with an arrow pointing right.

Peter's pulse quickened. Could that be where the Anti-Grav 500 was? Sure, he wanted to experience it with all the other expo attendees, but one quick peek right now wouldn't hurt.

He was about to go for it when something stopped him cold. An evil laugh echoed down the hall. The hairs on Peter's arms stood on end, but he didn't need his spider-sense to tell him something was wrong. He'd know that maniacal cackle anywhere. It was the Green Goblin! Which meant one thing–Spidey time!

Chapter 4

"At last," whispered a voice from behind a thick curtain that cloaked the wings of the stage. "Today is the day I add world domination to my villainous resume. Today I will make the Anti-Grav 500 mine. It will be the greatest weapon in my arsenal! My enemies will either follow me or float away." He cackled quietly then took a step toward the stage and the object of his desire. "All that stands between me and my new toy is a tiny glass case."

A finger tapped the Green
Goblin on the shoulder.

"And a human spider,"
Spider-Man said.

BAM! Spider-Man
delivered a mighty blow to
the Goblin's chest that sent
him flying. The green meanie
landed hard in a corner
backstage. He began to laugh.

The Green
Goblin was one
of Spidey's most
fearsome foes. They
had fought across
every one of New
York's five boroughs.
Though he was

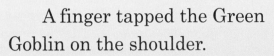

a madman, the Goblin was brilliant, which made defeating him that much more of a challenge.

"Spider-Boy," the Goblin said as he got to his feet. "You caught me off guard with a sucker punch. That isn't very honorable." He threw a spinning dagger at Spider-Man.

Spidey dodged it gracefully. "But stealing a priceless piece of technology is?" He shot his webs at the ceiling. "You're going to have to work with me on your definition of *honorable*."

Spider-Man grabbed his web and swung at the Goblin. The Goblin raised his hands and sent a blast of electricity from his gloves at the wall crawler. Spidey somersaulted out of the way. He landed on his feet and then charged his enemy. But before Spider-Man could reach him, the Goblin jumped onto his goblin glider. He zoomed onto the stage, smashed the glass case, and stole the Anti-Grav 500.

"HA-HA-HA-HA-HA!" the Goblin laughed. "Victory is mine! Victory is—*OOF!*"

"Short lived?" Spider-Man asked. His webs were coiled around the goblin glider, preventing it from flying away. "Now let's discuss your definition of *victory.*"

The Green Goblin turned to Spider-Man and grinned. He lifted the Anti-Grav 500. He pointed it at the wall crawler. And . . . *BLAST!*

The rays from the machine hit Spider-Man head on.

A lunatic laugh filled the auditorium. The Green Goblin draged his stalled glider and disappeared backstage, along with the anti-gravity laser.

Spider-Man did not chase after him. He couldn't. He was too busy floating away.

Chapter 5

The Amphitheatre was an open-air venue. That meant the only thing standing between the sky and a helpless, floating Super Hero was a tented roof that Spider-Man thought looked pretty flimsy.

Suddenly, a beam of energy zapped Spider-Man in the chest and his body descended to the ground. He landed safely on the floor of the stage where the Anti-Grav 500 had been.

A Super Hero dressed in red and blue with a gigantic left hand raced past. "Hi Spidey," Ms. Marvel called as she disappeared backstage. Another hero stood over Spider-Man holding the blaster that had returned his gravitational pull. She offered her hand to help him up.

"Captain Marvel!" Spider-Man said. "Thanks for the assist! The Green Goblin is here and I—"

"We know," Captain Marvel said. "Ms. Marvel is chasing him now. Which she wouldn't have had to do if you hadn't messed up our plan."

Spidey looked confused. "Your what now?"

Captain Marvel explained. "We knew the Goblin was coming for the Anti-Grav 500. That's why Ms. Marvel and I were patrolling the sky. If we didn't catch him on the way into the Amphitheatre, we were going to stop him on his way out."

Spider-Man smacked his forehead. "Aw, geez," he said. "I'm sorry."

Captain Marvel shrugged. "It's okay," she said. "We'll find him and then we'll put our plan back into action."

Spider-Man perked up. "I can help, too! I'm sort of an expert on the Green Goblin."

Captain Marvel looked skeptical.

"Seriously," Spidey said. "We're like arch enemies! I know everything about him. What weapons he uses. How he likes his tea (milk, two sugars). So, I know you've got your plan but—"

"Goblin incoming!" Ms. Marvel shouted.

Freed from Spider-Man's webs, the goblin glider sailed past Spidey and Captain Marvel. The Green Goblin cackled as he rode it into the afternoon sky. The Anti-Grav 500 was still in his hands.

Ms. Marvel jetted past them. "He's headed for the Cyclone!" she hollered, referring to the giant roller coaster on the boardwalk. She stretched farther and grew bigger with every step.

Spider-Man was about to join in the pursuit when Captain Marvel stopped him. "He's got the laser and we've got the blaster that reverses its effects. Ms. Marvel and I will handle this. Thanks anyway, Spider-Man," she said.

"But I can help!" he protested.

"Next battle," she said firmly. Then Captain Marvel fastened the gravitational blaster to her back and flew into the sky.

"Watch out for the delayed pumpkin bomb," Spider-Man called after her. "He loves to use it on newbies!" But she was already too far away to hear him.

Chapter 6

ZWISH!!

Mary Jane and Harry had just returned to the line and were looking for Peter when they saw the Green Goblin fly out of the Amphitheatre on a glider. In one hand he held a glowing pumpkin. In the other, the Anti-Grav 500.

"That's not good," Harry said.

MJ gasped. "We have to find Peter," she said. "We never should have split up. We never should have made him change his plans. And now we don't know where he is! What if he gets hurt? I feel terrible."

The Goblin turned and flew back toward the Amphitheatre. His madman's laugh rang out as he tore through the expo banner. MJ and Harry ducked.

"Don't feel terrible for Peter," Harry said. "Feel terrible for us! A Super Villain just flew over our heads!"

The Goblin zoomed down the boardwalk. He flew into the amusement park. "Time for a demonstration," he said. Then he lifted the Anti-Grav 500 and *BLAST!*

The laser hit the bumper cars where two friends, Lyra and Ayla, were enjoying their very first ride. They were happily ramming the other cars when their vehicle suddenly started to float. It was about to reach the ceiling when—*FZZT!*—another beam of light surrounded them and the car returned safely to the ground. The girls looked at each other wide-eyed.

"AGAIN!" they cheered.

From outside the Amphitheatre
MJ and Harry watched as two Super
Heroes chased the Green Goblin and
returned gravity to everything the
flying fink blasted.

"Harry, look!" MJ cried. "It's Ms.
Marvel and Captain Marvel. I *love*
them."

Harry clapped his hands. "We're
saved," he squealed. "Get 'em, Marvels!"

Chapter 7

"It's over, Goblin," Ms. Marvel said. She and Captain Marvel had him cornered against the Cyclone, right by the bumper cars. "Hand over the Anti-Grav 500 and we'll get you a knish for the ride to jail."

Just then an empty roller coaster car sped by on the track. The Green Goblin grabbed hold of it and was whisked away. "Catch me if you can!" he laughed.

Captain Marvel flew after him. Ms. Marvel stretched her limbs to cover more ground as she gave chase. The heroes followed the Goblin through every twist and turn, dip and drop of the Cyclone's wild ride. But when the coaster car reached the tippy top, the Goblin slammed on the brakes and yanked the car off its track.

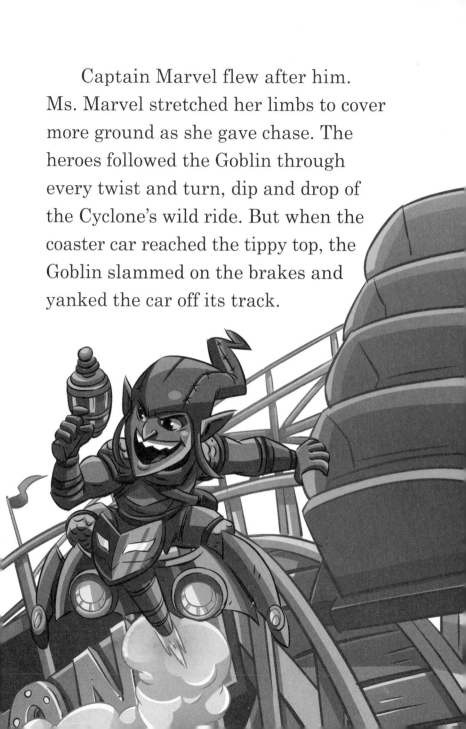

He turned to the Marvels and in a one-two punch, hurled the roller coaster car at Captain Marvel and a pumpkin bomb at Ms. Marvel.

"Embiggen!" Ms. Marvel yelled and her hand grew huge. She caught the pumpkin bomb in her fist and squeezed it to dust. "Crushed it!" she said.

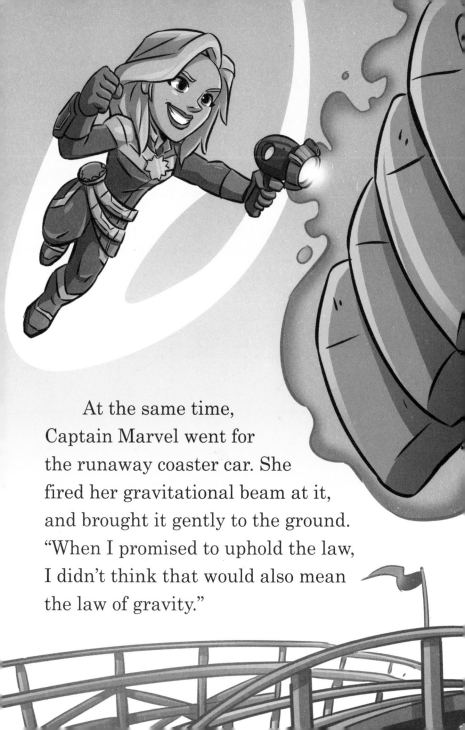

At the same time, Captain Marvel went for the runaway coaster car. She fired her gravitational beam at it, and brought it gently to the ground. "When I promised to uphold the law, I didn't think that would also mean the law of gravity."

The Marvels stood, fists raised, and faced the Green Goblin. He didn't hesitate. He hurled another pumpkin bomb in their direction, but it landed limp at their feet.

"Looks like this one is a dud," Captain Marvel said.

"That's what you think!" the Green Goblin cried.

BLAM!

The pumpkin bomb exploded. It knocked Ms. Marvel and Captain Marvel down and sent the gravitational blaster flying. It crashed onto the ground and broke into pieces.

As the Green Goblin took off down the boardwalk, a familiar figure ran to the heroes' aid. "Delayed pumpkin bomb, eh?" asked Spider-Man. He reached out his hands. "Maybe I can help."

Chapter 8

Spider-Man pulled Captain Marvel and Ms. Marvel to their feet.

"Boy are we glad to see you," Ms. Marvel said.

"Thank you, Spider-Man," added Captain Marvel. "It looks like we didn't know as much about the Green Goblin as we thought. Maybe our plan could have been a bit more flexible." She put her hand on the web-slinger's shoulder. "Think you could help us?"

Spidey said, "Anything for the Marvels."

Ms. Marvel clapped. "Ooooh, goodie! It's a team-up!"

"HA-HA-HA-HA-HA-HA!" The Goblin's evil laugh echoed down the boardwalk where he had left a trail of floating objects in his wake.

Captain Marvel lifted the pieces of the broken gravitational beam. "Think you two can contain the Goblin while I try to fix this? We'll need it if we want to reverse the effects of the Anti-Grav 500 and call this day saved."

"On it," Spidey and Ms. Marvel said in unison.

Then Ms. Marvel turned to Captain Marvel. They commenced their handshake. "Marvel me. Marvel you. Marvel Us!" they said.

Spider-Man smiled. "You're so going to have to teach me that," he said. Then he and Ms. Marvel hurried off down the boardwalk.

Captain Marvel got to work on the gravitational beam. In a matter of minutes, the machine was fixed except for one thing—the battery pack was missing.

Just then, she felt a tug on her arm. "Excuse me," Ayla from the bumper cars said.

"Are you looking for this?" asked her friend Lyra. Ayla held out her strawberry ice-cream cone for Captain Marvel to see. Stuck in the center of the creamy confection was the missing battery pack.

Captain Marvel high-fived the girls. "I sure am."

Chapter 9

Spider-Man and Ms. Marvel paused at the top of the boardwalk. Ahead of them was a path of floating people, pets, and things. A corn dog drifted past Spider-Man's face, followed by an ear of corn and an actual dog. "You don't see that every day," he said.

Ms. Marvel rubbed her forehead. "If Captain Marvel can fix her gravitational blaster, she can permanently reverse the effects of the Anti-Grav 500," she said. "So she'll bring everything that's floating away down safely. But we need to buy her some time. Think your webs are strong enough to keep stuff from floating into outer space?"

"There's only one way to find out," Spidey replied. *THWIP!* He shot a web at the floating dog and tied her to a post. The dog yipped and wagged her tail.

"It worked!" said Ms. Marvel. "Let's keep going!"

The heroes raced down the boardwalk. Rising above them were pretzels and pizzas, sideshow players and sunbathers. Even Spidey's old friend Officer Ditko was hanging around. "And I thought beach patrol would be relaxing," he said as the heroes shot past.

Spider-Man used his webs to tether anything that floated to something solid. Ms. Marvel used her stretchy arms to catch anything that drifted beyond the webs' reach.

Once all was secure, the heroes located the Goblin. "He's at the top of the parachute jump," Ms. Marvel said. "But how are we going to get up there without him using the laser on us?"

"I have an idea," said Spidey. "If there's one thing I know about the Green Goblin, it's that he loves to rub it in when he thinks he's won."

Ms. Marvel shook her head. "That's poor sportsmanship," she said.

"Sure is," Spider-Man agreed. "But what if we use that to our advantage? How are your acting skills?"

"Awesome," she replied. "I did a scene from *Frozen* for the Avengers talent show. Totally made Iron Man cry."

"Perfect," said Spidey. "If you can make the Goblin think he's got you beat, maybe you can distract him long enough for me to take him by surprise."

"Consider it done," Ms. Marvel said. And she was off and running before Spider-Man could say, "See you at the top."

Chapter 10

Ms. Marvel climbed up the spine of the parachute drop. She waved a little white flag. "Yoo hoo! Mr. Goblin," she called. "Are you up there?"

The Green Goblin flew down on his glider. He held the Anti-Grav 500 in his hand and was about to attack! But he paused when he saw the white flag of surrender.

"Oh, woe is me," Ms. Marvel began. "Green Goblin, you have me beat! It's time I admit defeat. You are too fast and too strong."

The Goblin looked at her suspiciously. Ms. Marvel held her breath. Then the Goblin settled into his glider. "And too clever," he added. "Don't forget too clever."

"And too clever," she agreed eagerly. She looked around. No Spider-Man yet. "You really are just so good at this bad guy thing. You're very—"

"Inspiring?" he asked.

"Totally inspiring!" Ms. Marvel cried. Still no Spidey. She continued to stall. "In fact, your, uh, success is making me consider a career change. Yeah, that's it. I want to be a bad guy!"

"Really?" The Goblin asked. "*I* made *you* want to be a villain?"

Suddenly, the Goblin felt a tap on his shoulder. He spun around to see Spider-Man hanging upside

of wind came up fr...
blew Spider-Man a...

"Okay, so that ...
to himself. He looke...
gulped. "Outer spac...
wanted to go there.

A bird flying ne...
take when she saw ...
Spider-Man whistle...
birdie, think I could ...
down to the boardw...
and I'll spring for so...

down behind him. "Nah," Spidey said. "But *she* did make *me* want to take acting lessons. Also, you have to stop falling for this."

WHAM!

Spider-Man knocked the Green Goblin out cold and straight off his glider. The bad guy flew down the boardwalk and landed in a car on the Wonder Wheel, where Officer Stanley and the NYPD were waiting.

"Nice job, S[...]
said. He did not[...]
She looked arou[...]
Spidey wasn't t[...]
up and gasped.[...]
the Anti-Grav 5[...]
the sky!

"I got the la[...]
"Unfortunately,[...]

"Hang tight[...]
She climbed to t[...]
parachute jump[...]
her body as long[...]
reaching for Spi[...]
foot. She almost[...]
of his toes when[...]

"I'm not a
big fan of peanuts,
but I wouldn't say no
to a cotton candy."

"Captain Marvel!"
Spider-Man cried as the
hero flew up beside him. "I
have never been so glad to see
someone—and her gravitational
blaster—in my life."

Captain Marvel aimed the beam
at Spider-Man and *FFZT!* She brought
him back down to the ground.

After the heroes restored gravity to
all the floating people and objects along

the boardwalk, they returned the Anti-Grav 500 to the science expo.

"Thanks for your help today, Spider-Man," Captain Marvel said. "I'm sorry I started out so stuck on my plan. Though having a plan is an important part of dealing with a problem, sometimes things change and we have to be able to change with them. Who knows? Sometimes the plan can get even better!"

"Believe it or not," said Spidey, "I totally understand." He thought of MJ and Harry and how he could have been more flexible with his own plan.

Ms. Marvel bounced excitedly. "Because you were such an awesome part of the team today, we thought we'd make you an honorary Marvel," she said. "Want to learn our handshake?"

Spider-Man gasped. The Marvels grinned. "Do I?!" he replied.

The trio wasted no time getting to work. Before long they perfected the handshake, complete with a special added twist.

"Marvel me. Marvel you. Marvel us! Excelsior!" they cried.

Captain Marvel threw her arm around Spider-Man's shoulder. "Now, about that cotton candy . . ."

Chapter
11

"Peter!" Mary Jane cried. She and Harry were standing outside the gates of Luna Park when she saw her missing friend approach. She ran to him and hugged him hard. "We are so glad to see you!"

"Yeah," Harry agreed. "Next time you storm off, make sure the Green Goblin isn't flying around zapping people with an anti-gravity laser. Okay?"

Peter laughed. "Okay," he agreed.

MJ pulled away and looked at the ground. "We're sorry we asked you to change your plans today," she said. "We knew how excited you were to see the Anti-Grav 500 and it stinks that you missed it."

"Oh, I got to see how it works," Peter said.

"Yeah, the Goblin put on quite a show," Harry agreed. "But really, Pete. We are sorry for messing up your plan."

Peter regarded his friends. "Thanks, guys, but I'm sorry, too," he said. "Things don't always go according to plan and that's okay. I'll try to be better at *going with the flow* from now on."

MJ linked her arm through Peter's. "Well, we've got a couple hours left before we have to head home. What do you want to do now?"

Peter thought about it. He shrugged and smiled. "I don't know," he said. "Let's just see what happens."

SPIDER-MAN AND MS. MARVEL IN MIGHTY MARVEL HANDSHAKE!

Hi! Want to become an honorary Marvel?

Trust me, it's awesome. I just became one a few pages ago.

You just have to learn the secret handshake. We'll walk you through it.

First, place your right hand over your heart.

This is when you say to your buddy, "Marvel Me."

Next comes the fist bump.

And this is when you say, "Marvel You."

Now grab hold of your friend's wrist. Like a handshake, but at the wrist.

Then say, "Marvel-Us!"

And finally, shoot your arms up into the sky and do a Spidey thwip!

And yell out, "Excelsior!"

That's all there is to it! Now you're an honorary Marvel.

Teach it to your friends and start your own Marvel Team-Up.

We'll see you next time! Until then, stay marvelous!